MW00953684

MJ'S NEW FRIEND
BY JUDY ANN LOWE

ILLUSTRATED BY AYUNA COLLINS AND DAVID EDWARD MARTIN

J.S. Pathways
Dallas, Texas

© Copyright 2014 Judy Ann Lowe   All Rights Reserved

No part of this publication may be reproduced or transmitted or utilized in any form or by any means, electronic, mechanical, photocopying or otherwise, without the prior permission of the author.

Illustrations by Ayuna Collins and David Edward Martin

Design by Carolyn Oakley, Luminous Moon Design

Published by J.S. Pathways

Printed in the United States

ISBN-13: 978-1499139679
ISBN-10: 1499139675

Dedication

To my loving husband and soul mate Sam,
to whom I am so grateful for awakening me to the truth
that there are people of higher awareness
on other planets.

MJ, wearing his favorite blue and orange soccer uniform, was watching the other boys practicing their soccer moves. The boys really liked kicking the ball and competing against each other. MJ was taking a break after playing very hard with them.

He looked away from the practice and saw a new boy standing all alone. The boy looked puzzled, watching the other kids running after the ball. MJ had never seen him on the soccer field before. He walked over to the boy to greet him.

"What's your name?" MJ asked the boy.

"My name's Vebo," the young boy answered. "What's yours?"

"My name is MJ."

The boys smiled at each other.

MJ could tell that there was something special about Vebo. He wasn't afraid of him, just curious. Vebo didn't look much different from the other boys MJ knew at school. He had blond hair, violet eyes that were a little bigger than usual, and a kind face. MJ liked Vebo because he was so nice and very friendly.

The soccer coach blew his whistle to let
everyone know that soccer practice was over.
As everyone started to leave, MJ looked back
at Vebo and waved goodbye to him.

The next day, MJ hoped he would see Vebo again
during soccer practice, but he wasn't there. After a few
days, MJ still hadn't seen him again. He realized that he
missed his new friend a lot.

Then a week later, MJ saw Vebo on the playground. Vebo was wearing a curious-looking jacket. It was made of an iridescent fabric with unusual symbols on the collar wrap. The symbols kept changing! MJ wondered what the symbols meant and if the jacket would even glow in the dark.

"Where have you been, Vebo," MJ asked. "I missed you. And where did you get that jacket? It's so cool."

"I brought it back from visiting my family and friends who live very far away. It's my favorite thing to wear."

MJ nodded his head because he thought he understood. "It's an awesome jacket. I have family who lives far away also. They live all the way in California!"

Vebo just smiled. He looked back at the other boys, who were playing with the ball again. He finally asked MJ, "What IS that ball thing?"

"It's a game called soccer," MJ said. He was surprised that Vebo hadn't seen or heard of soccer.

Vebo wanted to know more about it, so MJ excitedly started telling him all about the game. Soccer was MJ's favorite sport. He loved playing, watching and talking about it.

The other boys stopped playing and watched the two of them and then joined in. Soon they were all showing Vebo soccer moves.

Vebo learned fast. He learned the rules of the game, dribbling, passing and goalkeeping. The boys even showed him some fancy soccer tricks. He was making more friends now besides MJ.

MJ wanted to let Vebo have a chance to maneuver the ball.

"Here Vebo," MJ said, passing him the ball. "Now it's your turn."

When Vebo touched the ball with his foot, a beautiful circle of pale, colored light surrounded the ball like tiny rainbow colors and then disappeared within the blink of an eye. A few of the other people actually saw this special moment in time. They had never seen anything like that before.

As they watched the ball, it disappeared and suddenly reappeared down the field. Everyone was amazed and a little afraid.

MJ and the boys all started talking at once.

"How did you DO that?"

"OH MY GOSH!"

"That's incredible!"

"Duuuude!"

"I'm a little different from you because I come from a different star system," Vebo told them calmly. "It is called the Pleiades and it is a friendly and peaceful place."

The boys gasped and stepped back from Vebo. They didn't know what to think about this.

MJ stepped up beside Vebo. "You may be different from us, but you're my best friend. You're way cool and totally trustworthy. I know we can always count on you."

MJ could tell the boys and other people were really listening to what he was saying. He looked at Vebo, who was smiling back at him.

MJ told him he was glad he was here. The other boys agreed.

They wanted to know everything about Vebo and what life was like on a different planet, because it sounded so cool.

"Do you have swimming pools?"

"Do you play soccer?"

"What do you eat and drink?"

"Do you have soda pop?"

"What about ice cream?"

"And, what about pizza?"

But the most important thing to them at the moment was how could they do what Vebo did when he touched the soccer ball with his foot and how could they get to be as good as Vebo?

One of the boys asked him, "Can you teach us how to do that, too?"

"Yes, of course!" Vebo told them. "We can all work together and learn extraordinary things from each other."

As the day came to a close and the sun went down, the stars began to come out. Vebo looked up and saw the stars representing the Pleiades star cluster. Now that he was officially a member of the team, he felt very at ease around MJ and the boys. He showed them the stars of his home and told them all about life on the Pleiades.

This was just the beginning of a great friendship for MJ, Vebo and the boys. It was also the beginning of a truly amazing learning experience for them all—and that was a good thing!

THE PLEIADES

The Pleiades are part of a larger group of stars called the Taurus constellation, or the Seven Sisters and their parents Pleione and Atlas. It is the best known open star cluster. There are approximately 1,000 or more stars in the Pleiades star cluster. However, only six of them can be seen easily without a telescope. The Pleiades are best seen during the winter season, between September and November, for those people who live in the Northern Hemisphere and sometimes in the Southern Hemisphere because that is when they reach their highest point in the sky. For many other places on Earth, the Pleiades are visible from mid-June to early May.

The star cluster is controlled by hot blue and extremely luminous stars that have formed within the last 100 million years. The Pleiades are more than 400 light-years from Earth and the rest of the solar system. Galileo was the first astronomer to study the Pleiades through a telescope.

Along with many other ancient myths, the legend of the Pleiades helps children understand acts of courage, love, loyalty, strength, perseverance, leadership, self reliance, how to act and behave, and other important life lessons.

Acknowledgments

With great appreciation to:
Carolyn Oakley for her expertise with book layout and creative direction; Ayuna Collins and David Edward Martin for their artistic creativity; and Karen Gresham Nickell for her unending support, ideas and motivation.

ABOUT THE AUTHOR

Judy Lowe is a retired Gifted and Talented teacher in the Dallas Independent School District in Dallas, Texas. Since 1966, she has earned a Bachelor's Degree in Music Education, a Masters Degree in Elementary Education and a Certificate in Gifted and Talented Education. Her hobbies are reading, working in the yard, walking, and being outside.

Judy enjoys musicals, attending The Vocal Majority performances, traveling, and watching many programs on PBS, the Hallmark Channel and the History Channel. She currently serves on the Board of Directors of the North Texas Book Festival, Inc. and is a member of the Dallas Museum of Art, Texas Retired Teachers Association, Dallas ISD TAG Educators Alumni, KERA, and the Texas Association of Authors.

The inspiration for this story came from Judy's husband, Sam, who had an interest in UFOs and people from other planets.

It is Judy's desire that children of all ages open their hearts to those who are a little different. Our beautiful planet Earth will only evolve through love and light. ☮

Visit Judy online at www.JSPathways.com and
Facebook.com/JSPathways

ABOUT THE ARTISTS

Ayuna Collins and David E. Martin live and work in Los Angeles, California. While both have independent art careers, they also work as a collaborative, multimedia illustration team. Their differing backgrounds operates as a key component in their creation process. The team often works on several pieces at once, trading back and forth, each adding the next layer or element until the picture has come to life.

Ayuna Collins earned her undergraduate degree in dance and animation at California Institute of the Arts. Her masters focuses on where a lack of memory and the artistic practice meet.

David Edward Martin is an artist and educator. Trained in filmmaking and motion graphics, he seeks out the nuanced connections between various modes of expression.

Enjoy these other magical titles by Judy Ann Lowe!

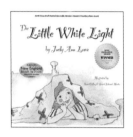  

Available at Amazon.com, BarnesandNoble.com,
4BR.store and from the publisher at JSPathways.com

Learn more about Judy's books, see a schedule of her upcoming events, and
enjoy videos and photos at JSPathways.com and Facebook.com/JSPathways

Made in the USA
Middletown, DE
09 September 2022

10004061R00018